A TWIST IN THE TALE

Edited by Lucy Jenkins

First published in Great Britain in 2000 by
YOUNG WRITERS
Remus House,
Coltsfoot Drive,
Woodston,
Peterborough, PE2 9JX
Telephone (01733) 890066

All Rights Reserved

Copyright Contributors 1999

HB ISBN 0 75431 729 3
SB ISBN 0 75431 730 7

FOREWORD

This year, for the first time ever, Young Writers proudly presents a showcase of the best mini sagas from over 2,500 up-and-coming writers nationwide.

To write a mini saga - a story told in only fifty words - much imagination and skill is required. *A Twist In The Tale* achieves and excels these requirements and this exciting anthology will not disappoint the reader.

The thought, effect and hard work put into each mini saga impressed us all and the task of editing proved challenging due to the quality of entries received, but was nevertheless enjoyable. We hope you are as pleased as we are with the final selection and that you continue to enjoy *A Twist In The Tale* for many years to come.

CONTENTS

The End Of A Knight	Dominic O'Dair	1
Mysterious Stranger	Rebecca J Gisborne	2
The Happenning	Anne-Marie Donnelly	3
Killer Instinct	Emma Crosby	4
Hide And Seek	Louise Bennett	5
The Court Surprise	Jessica Taroni	6
The Reckless Adventure	Rebecca Leggatt	7
The Lifetime Experience	Shane Geoghegan	8
The Chase	William Cowley	9
Burnt	Rebecca White	10
Pain And Glory	Gavin McKenna	11
Get Away!	Sophie Perkins	12
The Secret Treasure	Rebecca Le Maitre	13
Smile!	Holly Somers	14
Please Mind The Gap . . .	Hazel Davies	15
The Scariest Few Minutes Of My Life	Josh Fry	16
Penalty!	Jan Oles	17
Extraordinary Eclipse of 1999	Catherine Fagg	18
Darkness	Zoe Adams	19
Ice-Cool Alex	Richard Radford	20
Mirror Image	Emily Moseley	21
The Dragon	Aleisha Dawes	22
1st Place	Roxy Thorpe	23
The Eclipse	Inderpal Singh Reehal	24
A Twist In The Tale	James Hancock	25
Pursuit	Joanna Parry	26
Terror Of The Unknown	Claire Metcalfe	27
Stolen Dreams	Sophie Evans	28
Revenge Of The Moon	Kimberley Wrigley	29
Don't Be Silly	Sarah Sheldon	30
Did The World End Or Not?	Sally Thompson	31
It's All Up To Me	Sophie Bowsher	32
Secret Encounter	Nicholas Moore	33
Jaws	Jessica Hughes	34
Teatime Surprise	Kirsty Smyth	35

Meal Or Murder?	Amy Hall	36
The Serengeti	Amy Gathercole	37
Eclipse	Rachelle Forrest	38
Love At First Sight	Chris Williams	39
The Chase	Kelly Weldin	40
Phew!	Rotha Satterthwaite	41
My Cornish Eclipse From Home	Nick Humphrey	42
What Is It?	Jennifer Hartley	43
A Snail's Race	Samantha Watkins	44
The Chase	Peter Simpson	45
Was History About To Be Made?	Emma Hammond	46
Screaming In The 'Torture Chamber'	Nicole Lynch	47
The Third And Final Cup	Adam Duncan	48
Today Is The Day	Michael Doherty	49
First Day At Nursery School	Jennifer Nesbitt	50
Pony Power	Rachel Ervine	51
Silent Schoolroom	Jessica Greer	52
The Moth	Aidan Garvey	53
Scared Silly	Chrissie Kidd	54
Buried Treasure	Ruth Mulvenna	55
Spine-Chillers	Isabella Spagnuolo	56
The Day The Sun Went Out	Zerrin Djemil	57
The Strange Tale	Isheeta Gor	58
À La Carte Cuisine	Helen Ritchie	59
The Race	Louise Foy	60
Dancing With . . .	Megan Nannfeldt	61
Murder In The Dark	Karla Thurston	62
Run	Rebekah Rocker	63
A Mysterious Teacher With A Deadly Secret	Jay Shetty	64
The End Of The World!	Deborah Rouse	65
The Scene	Andrew Oduro Ayim	66
The Cave	Joanna Odei Frimpong	67
Nightmare	Timothy Gibson	68
Vahawk	Joel Williams	69

You Will Never See Your Mother Again	Ayodele Cameron	70
The Dead End	Kerry McKenzie	71
The Sea Monster	Lisa Clavey	72
The Eclipse	Carly Forster	73
They're Out	Siobhan Hughes	74
Final Moments	Jack Robinson	75
Burgled Or Not!	Eleanor Jane Hopkins	76
Desperate To Go	Stephanie Jayson	77
Approach With Caution	Michaela McQueeney	78
Trouble	Samantha Lustig	79
On The Field	Georgina Whitehead	80
Raging Seas	Timothy Scargill	81
Nervous	Sarah Sultana	82
Near-Death Experience	Andrew Barklam	83
Fears	Emily Brown	84
Eclipse	Matthew Mullen	85
China's First Impression Of The Eclipse	Emma Chandley	86
Going To The Dentist	Helen Alexander	87
On The Run	Siân Humphries	88
No Escaping	Fiona Kelly	89
Mysterious Footsteps	Hannah Tickle	90
The Killing	Joanne Allen	91
Fishing	Bernice Connell	92
Winter	Kayleigh Nash	93
The Shuttlecock Catastrophe	Ian Copeland	94
Kidnapped	Amy Briggs	95
Tiger Trouble	Andrew Barrett	96
The Monster That Ate The Sun	Stephen Mitchell	97
Footsteps	Rachel Price	98
Mystery Of The Deep	Peter Willis	99
Scared Of Water?	Catherine Porter	100
A Cold Touch	Rachael Hilderley	101
The Rose	Rhiannon Burgess	102
The Most Amazing Experience Of Our Life	Beccy Rolland	103
Carelessness	Emily Read	104

The Demon From The Dark Side	Emily Cawston-Rollin	105
Mini Saga	Charlotte Burton	106
Shadows	Harriet Newcombe	107
Cold-Blooded Killer	Cara George	108
Worries	Bryannie Drury	109
Running, Running	Roxanne Evans	110
Mini Saga	Kelly Parkhouse	111
The Warm Presence	Hayley Dixon	112
Ferocious Monster	Nicola Kirby	113
That Book!	Laura Gatehouse	114
The Race	Karl Hayman	115
The Gargoyle	Cherith Webb	116
The Victim	Tamsyn Lee	117
On The Back Of A Hawk	Victoria Evans	118
The Earthquake	Cassie Specterman	119
The Shot	Lauren Webster	120
Mini Saga	Aiza Arshad	121
Suddenly Come . . . Suddenly Gone?	Jennifer Coughlin	122
My Mini Saga	Francesca Blake	123
Eclipsed	Nealey Swadkins	124
The Bar	Rosie Dymock	125
The Rising Monster	Christopher Baker	126
Mini Saga	Ayesha Malik	127
The Challenge	Elizabeth Williams	128
Betrayal	Zoë Copson	129
Tense Moments	John DeBoo	130
The Mysterious Figure	Danielle Lowis	131
My Sister Needs Help!	Rebecca Wall	132
A Glimpse Of The Beastie	Paul Harrison	133
The Battle Of The Middle Ages	Michael Myers	134
Tears In My Eyes	Kerry Taplin	135
Paradise	Jennifer Baldwin	136
Fair Dues	Alison Seal	137
In The Kitchen	Nadia Schramm	138
The Halt	Faye-Marie Cryer	139
The Dentist	Kathryn McCandless	140
Bedroom Horror	Kathryn Elizabeth Callow	141

Don't Let The Sun Get In Your Eyes, Don't let . . .	Diarmuid Tejero-White	142
Jewels!	Naomi Crewe	143
Eclipse	Thomas Zacharchenko	144
Waiting For The Chance	Deborah Lomax	145
A Madman's Obsession	Ben Fish	146
Angst	Nazneen Tabassum	147
The Dreaded Moment	Nadia Yousuf	148
Splash!	Jamie Linnell	149
Strangely Familiar	David Kelley	150
To My Surprise	Hayley Sharman	151
A Tiger's Teatime	Corrine Kaenzig	152
The Nightly Menace	Sara Bentley	153
The Kiss	Laura Saggars	154
The Star	Leah Mann	155
Razor Blades	Charlotte Low	156
The Sound Of Water	Charlotte Shannon-Little	157
Sudden Darkness	Hannah Clark	158
Mini Saga	Michael Addinell	159
Honk	Rhiannon Byers	160
Love	Rachel Krengel	161
The Shadow!	Georgiana Simmons	162
All Is Not What It Seems . . .	Shelley Greenwood	163
Alternate Exercise	Elissa Rose	164
Alone In The Dark	Liam Paul Murphy	165
The Battle	Charlotte Hawksley	166

The Mini Sagas

THE END OF A KNIGHT

The cold steel painted a cruel slash across my cheek. A droplet of blood trickled down my face and splashed onto the decaying wood-slatted floor. The knight raised his rapier again to strike me and there was no way out . . .

'Time for school, honey,' Mum called from downstairs.

Dominic O'Dair (11)

MYSTERIOUS STRANGER

I stood on the cliff staring out to the misty sea
I could see the waves crashing against the
Rocks, and the wind sweeping the
Sand across the beach.
There was a man sitting on the sand,
He looked up, smiled and mist descended on
Him and he faded away.

Rebecca J Gisborne (11)

THE HAPPENING

I sat waiting, waiting for the cry, the scream
and the sound of the happening.
After ten minutes, a cry of pain as it began to start.
Ten minutes later, what we had all been waiting for.
After months of waiting and hours of pain,
finally the baby was born.

Anne-Marie Donnelly (11)

KILLER INSTINCT

Like a statue he stood motionless,
hidden from view by a cluster of bushes.
His eyes gleaming as they followed every move
of his victim, a short distance away.
Sure that his moment was right,
he sprang, ready for the kill.
The bird, catching sight of the cat,
took flight.

Emma Crosby (11)

HIDE AND SEEK

I hid behind a bush,
I could hear footsteps coming closer.
I didn't move, I froze.
What would I do?
I made up my mind,
I ran as fast as I could across the soggy ground.
I felt him behind me, but I made it,
He didn't find me.

Louise Bennett (11)

THE COURT SURPRISE!

I woke up, my heart pounding.
What will it be like?
My first time in court.
I sat there looking around the room.
Was everyone staring at me,
Or was it my imagination?
We were told to stand, the judge entered.
Father looked so different in a cloak and wig.

Jessica Taroni (11)

THE RECKLESS ADVENTURE

He endlessly climbed twisted scraps of metal,
towards a prodigious heap of deformed blue.
Sitting at the top, exhausted from his strenuous mount,
a bloodcurdling scream echoed throughout the jungle.
He'd slipped and had skidded to the bottom.

> My brother then stood up
> and ran towards the slide again!

Rebecca Leggatt (11)

THE LIFETIME EXPERIENCE

As it moved into position,
I felt the ice-cold air settle in,
hitting my warm face, sending me a shiver.

The amount of light
dropping dramatically.

It kept getting more and more quiet,
till silence.

The sun was covered, then *flash*,
the beautiful corona was shown.

Shane Geoghegan (11)

THE CHASE

The mass of foliage blocked out the light.
I could feel heavy breathing on the back of my neck.
I ran faster and faster. The 'thing' behind me gave chase.
Past trees and through swamps, the chase ensued.
A clammy hand grabbed my shoulder!
'Tag, you're it!'

William Cowley (11)

BURNT

The smoke slowly made shapes,
above the glowing embers.
Animal fat dribbled onto a blazing fire,
flames rose uncontrollably into the warm breeze,
and once again . . .
Dad burnt the sausages on the barbecue.

Rebecca White (11)

PAIN AND GLORY

Soaring through the air at a tremendous speed,
I feel like I have been shot with a million bullets.
Falling to my knees in total pain with blood
gushing like a stream.

The cricket ball had hit me in the mouth
and then fallen into my hand.
I shouted . . . 'Howzat'

Gavin McKenna (11)

GET AWAY!

I fell to the ground. He was getting closer. I got up and dragged myself along. I was determined to get away. I came to a dead end. I turned and saw him. There was only a fence between freedom and me. I pulled myself over. I was free!

Sophie Perkins (11)

THE SECRET TREASURE

Me and my three mates went rock climbing
while our parents were chatting.

Near the top we saw a huge rock,
we scrambled behind it.

There our eyes sparkled with joy, my heart pounded,
it was a shiny pile of gold coins.
We shared it out and there we became rich.

Rebecca Le Maitre (11)

SMILE!

I wouldn't. Never.
They couldn't make me.
I was determined not to give in.
I stood there glaring at the photographer,
a frown glued to my face.
'Smile,' he beamed.
The frown began to unpeel,
I couldn't stop it.
The corners of my mouth lifted,
I was . . . smiling.

Holly Somers (11)

PLEASE MIND THE GAP . . .

The black worm comes slithering down the tunnel,
whining and roaring as it comes.

It slows down, with a hiss, a jolt, a splutter.
From the slits in its sides, I can see light.

Another hiss, a door opens. A door?
People spill out. I blink. I hate undergrounds.

Hazel Davies (11)

THE SCARIEST FEW MINUTES OF MY LIFE

My head was spinning, screams
and shouts of fellow victims petrified me,
bright lights dazzled all around
and there was a thumping in my ears.
A dark figure came towards our great capsule.
He grabbed at it bringing us to a halt.
'Congratulations daring young lads,
you survived the waltzers!'

Josh Fry (11)

PENALTY!

A shiver penetrated my trembling body.
I tried desperately not to close my eyes.
I felt a force like a ten ton weight crushing my body.
Instantly I fell to the ground clutching the weight to my chest.
The next thing I knew a voice cried 'What a brilliant save.'

Jan Oles (11)

EXTRAORDINARY ECLIPSE OF 1999

It came rushing towards the gathering crowd. The shadow covered the anxious spectators. The birds stopped singing and the air cooled as the darkness crept in. Then it began to get lighter again. Everyone cheered. A moving sight for all watchers.

It was the last *total eclipse* of the millennium!

Catherine Fagg (11)

DARKNESS

Everybody was stood still looking in the same direction with their dark glasses on. Gradually it got darker and darker. From the darkness shone a circle of light.

A sigh of amazement spread through the crowd. Then slowly the moon passed the sun and the total eclipse was over.

Zoe Adams (11)

ICE-COOL ALEX

Alex Dawson was up against one of the roughest defenders in the game, Graham Hunter. All match Hunter fouled Dawson, but he was not put off by Hunter's tactics. Dawson got the ball on the edge of the box, shot to the keeper's right and *scored*. Full-time, 1-0!

Richard Radford (11)

MIRROR IMAGE

She looked into the mirror, wonder in her sparkly, green emerald eyes. Her bright blood-red lips opened slightly as her flushed cheeks gave warmth to her features. There she stood, staring into the mirrored glass. The black dress fitted nicely. The diet had worked!

Emily Moseley (11)

THE DRAGON

The boy watched the dragon fly
through the sky reaching to the sun.
Its wings were billowing in the wind,
as its nostrils flared.
Fire from the dragon shoots across the sky.
His scaly neck reaches high in the clouds.
'Time to go home!'
The boy reeled in his kite.

Aleisha Dawes (11)

1ST PLACE

Bang! Everyone cheered as the beanbags went into the hoops.
Then there was silence. One beanbag missed, it went over.
She tried again, it went in. Everyone screamed 'Yes, go!'
She dodged the cones, picked up the skipping rope and skipped.
She saw the finish line. She won!

Roxy Thorpe (11)

THE ECLIPSE

It all went dark,
It had begun.
The temperature dropped,
There was an eerie feeling all around.
The moon came over the sun.
Silence all over the country.
You finally saw the sun.
There was an outbreak of applause.
The eclipse had just occurred.

Inderpal Singh Reehal (11)

A Twist In The Tale

There was a shady figure standing
at the bottom of the path.
He walked up to me then paused.
He reached for his bag dangling from his shoulder,
put his hand inside and pulled out a small,
square-looking package and said . . .
'That's all the post for today!'

James Hancock (11)

PURSUIT

I ran as fast as I could, galloping and leaping
over many objects that stood in my way,
hiding behind huge trunks in the dark forest
where he had been chasing me.
He passed, the wind blew my scraggy hair.
Then a scaly hand clenched my shoulder
tightly and squeezed.

Joanna Parry (11)

TERROR OF THE UNKNOWN

Our spy was sent out. He was entering the danger zone.
We waited until cautiously, he signalled.
We rushed to our places, the ones we had rehearsed so many times.
The enemy began to approach, thundering closer and closer.
We stayed perfectly still . . . she was here.
'Good morning Miss.'

Claire Metcalfe (11)

STOLEN DREAMS

The jewels were in sight but in a glass case surrounded by lasers.
If I put one foot wrong I would set off the alarms.
Carefully I threaded my body through the beams towards the jewels.
As I got closer I stumbled, the alarms buzzed
and Mum shouted 'Get up!'

Sophie Evans (11)

REVENGE OF THE MOON

It was about to happen
and everyone knew it.
It started to move,
slowly it got dark,
the sun had a shadow
going in its path.
It had begun,
the moon took over,
the sun had died.
The moon had won the battle,
but the sun came back to life.

Kimberley Wrigley (11)

DON'T BE SILLY

Walking into the bank he took a gun out of his pocket.
'This is a stick-up! Hand over your money, no one will get hurt.'
Everyone ignored the man, frustrated he looked down,
to his horror he realised that he hadn't taken the red end
off his plastic pop gun.

Sarah Sheldon (11)

DID THE WORLD END OR NOT?

Whilst in the garden reading about Nostradamus predicting the end of the world, the light faded suddenly. The temperature dropped, it became deadly quiet. I felt scared. I thought this was the world ending.

Suddenly it was brighter and warmer. My watch read 11.13am, 11.8.99. This was the eclipse.

Sally Thompson (11)

IT'S ALL UP TO ME

All eyes were on me, every face of every person
glared at me, they were all depending on me.
I felt if I let them down I would let the whole town down.
My heart was beating fast, it sounded like someone humming.
I kicked the ball and scored.
Goal!

Sophie Bowsher (11)

SECRET ENCOUNTER

Slowly and secretly he planned his approach. The grass quivered creating a faint noise. Had he been heard? No. Quietly he moved closer and closer. A leaf rustled . . . He had been heard. It was now or never. Instantly he pounced. The weasel hung limply from the snake's fangs.

Nicholas Moore (11)

JAWS

Jaws swam majestically through the water,
searching . . . searching.
His eyes glistening as he spotted his prey.
With deliberate, yet graceful movements,
he motioned towards his goal and then paused,
waiting for the moment that he would seize.
Then . . . snap!
Yes, it was feeding time for Jaws, my pet goldfish.

Jessica Hughes (11)

TEATIME SURPRISE

I walked through the big black gate
and over the long, twirling cobbly path
to a big black door with cobwebs hanging.
I knocked on it - thud, thud, thud.
Squeeak!
The door opened slowly,
a big shadow came to my feet.
'Is my tea ready Mum?' I said.

Kirsty Smyth (11)

MEAL OR MURDER?

The murderer creeps up on the victim who's unaware that its life will be cut short. Stealthily and carefully he moves, keeping his eye on the victim. Then he thinks 'Is it worth the trouble?' Then he thinks, 'It's my tea isn't it?' Whiskers pounces on the unknowing rabbit.

Amy Hall (11)

THE SERENGETI

Prowling through the long brown grass,
as silent as a mouse.
The powerful lion stalks his prey.
Unaware, the graceful antelope stands
chomping the dew soaked grass.
Suddenly he makes his move.
The graceful antelope spots him.
The antelope isn't as skilful as the lion.
He didn't stand a chance.

Amy Gathercole (11)

ECLIPSE

Sarah and her family waited outside for the moment to arrive, then the whole family watched with amazement as darkness crept over the sky.
There was silence and a chill gripped the air,
everybody was so excited, they all gave a big cheer.
It was a moment to remember . . . forever.

Rachelle Forrest (11)

LOVE AT FIRST SIGHT

She walked past me,
like a heatwave on a hot day.
My heart was racing as never before,
I raised my hand to my face and slapped myself!
'Get a grip,' I said.
It's just a *girl!*

Chris Williams (11)

THE CHASE

She was after me.
Only a few metres behind . . .
Getting closer.
Her sharp claws scraping my back.
A spurt of energy rushes through me
as I speed on,
only to end in failure.
I trip.
She sprints ahead
towards the finish line.
I have lost the race.
To my grandma!

Kelly Weldin (11)

PHEW!

There was a giggle, then it all went *black*. The lights had gone out! Alison turned on a torch. She held it to her face. It cast eerie shadows. She started telling a ghost story. The door opened. We froze. The light came on, and ... phew ... It's only Mum!

Rotha Satterthwaite (11)

MY CORNISH ECLIPSE FROM HOME

Slowly the moon covered the sun.
First - the first touch;
second - partial eclipse;
last - the experience of a lifetime:
Total eclipse.
The sky turned blacker, blacker,
until it was dark as dusk,
dark as you will ever see before
midday.
Bats approaching from nowhere,
seagulls, crows returning to their nests.

Nick Humphrey (11)

WHAT IS IT?

It was dark.
I heard footsteps on the stairs.
Stertorous breathing coming closer.
Suddenly I was pinned down.
Panic! Where am I? What is happening?
Something wet and slimy dribbled onto my cheek.
A dark face peered under the bedclothes.
Relief! It was my boxer dog 'Holly'!

Jennifer Hartley (11)

A Snail's Race

Going towards the start line slowly, I'm a snail.
I'm racing a slug, because he said I'm slower.
Bang! We're off. Across the slab, slug's leading.
Over the stone, we're even.
Moving past the cat, slug's been caught!
I'm winning! What's that shadow above me?
'Dad, you've squashed the snail!'

Samantha Watkins (11)

THE CHASE

I ran through the courtyard and through the house,
wondering where it could be.
I'd been chasing for a while now,
then I saw it in the bushes, covered in mud.
I had to get it, everything felt very tense.
I pounced out and grabbed it and said
'Tag, you're it!'

Peter Simpson (11)

WAS HISTORY ABOUT TO BE MADE?

I stood there excited, my heart beating double.
The sky then grew darker.
Was I in trouble?
All around me people clapped and cheered.
Was history about to be made?
Suddenly it happened,
I couldn't believe it!
Such excitement filled the air.
'The eclipse!' I shouted.

Emma Hammond (11)

SCREAMING IN THE 'TORTURE CHAMBER'

I was put into the room.
The door closed swiftly behind.
I was petrified, heart pounding.
What were they going to do to me?
What gruesome instruments waited for me
in the torture chamber?
I heard a click.
Suddenly the door opened.
'Miss Lynch, the dentist is ready for you!'

Nicole Lynch (11)

THE THIRD AND FINAL CUP

Ninety minutes passed.
Nothing.
'We're finished,' I said.
We needed a miracle or a new lease of life.
Injury time and two fresh men.
With hearts pounding we watched.
One and then *two*.
We are now the *champions*
three times over.

Adam Duncan (11)

TODAY IS THE DAY

Today is the day.
Some of us thought it was all over,
but I knew the torment would continue.
I put on the familiar clothing,
I had worn many times before.
Then words which struck fear in my heart,
were said.
'Time for school,' my mum said.

Michael Doherty (11)

FIRST DAY AT NURSERY SCHOOL

He leaves his sanctuary,
his hand gripping tightly,
he begins a journey.
He tries to run,
he struggles and screams,
but all in vain.
He approaches a small building,
the door opens.
No! No!
He yells,
but he is pulled inside.
Smiling faces,
colourful walls.
Maybe it's not so bad!

Jennifer Nesbitt (11)

PONY POWER

I was playing in the field.
Suddenly I heard hooves galloping towards me.
I looked back but could see nothing.
I started to run, the drumming of the hooves
grew louder and louder.
I felt panic stricken, I looked up.
Magic, my pony, gazed down at me, puzzled.

Rachel Ervine (11)

SILENT SCHOOLROOM

Only the scratch or inky flow of writing pervaded the absolute quiet. Pens moved mechanically over pages filled with endless handwritten words.

One pen was motionless. Its owner sat, watching constantly the steadily falling snowflakes outside, his concentration utterly absent from that silent schoolroom.

Then he started, realising he was alone.

Jessica Greer (11)

THE MOTH

There I lay in my bed frightened because the darkness had come without any warning. Suddenly a gust of wind came through the window and slammed the door shut. I couldn't hear or see anything. Something touched my nose and buzzed round my face. It was that moth again.

Aidan Garvey (11)

SCARED SILLY

I was quietly watching what was going on.
Looked to my left then my right.
Two scary men coming towards me with guns!
What should I do? Duck or run?
Squirt, squirt water everywhere.
I didn't know they squirted each other with water.
I'd never been to a circus before.

Chrissie Kidd (11)

BURIED TREASURE

I had been looking for the buried treasure for ages,
but I kept going as I heard footsteps and shouting behind me.
The longing of this moment was unbearable.
I saw the corner of the box sticking out.
I opened it, there it sat.
My gold - a bar of chocolate.

Ruth Mulvenna (11)

SPINE-CHILLERS

The dreadful ghost stood quite still in the pale moonlight. He was an old man of terrible appearance. His eyes were as red as burning coals. Long grey hair fell over his hunched shoulders. From his bony wrists hung the rusty chains. 'Dad! Get that white sheet off you.'

Isabella Spagnuolo (11)

THE DAY THE SUN WENT OUT

It was a bright, sunny Wednesday. Me and my mum went to the garden to watch the amazing event. Then it happened, the first time I'd seen it. It was fantastic! Afterwards, it was cold and gloomy. The world was eerie and silent. It was a *total eclipse!*

Zerrin Djemil (11)

THE STRANGE TALE

Sarah was looking at stars in her garden when a star came shooting down at her. She caught it in her hands. A face appeared on it. 'I need an ivory leaf,' it said. Sarah gave the star the leaf and it went back into the sky. 'Thank you,' it said.

Isheeta Gor (11)

À LA CARTE CUISINE

There it was buzzing round her head again.
'Oh goodie, it's back!' she croaked eagerly.
The unwary victim settled on a gnarled twig nearby,
not knowing the uncertainty of its predicament.
The predator moved gradually closer.
'Thlwap!' out went the tongue and in went the bluebottle.
'Mmm . . . very tasty.'

Helen Ritchie (11)

THE RACE

Faster and faster, the racing cars zoomed around the circuit, so fast they seemed out of control. Suddenly the leading green car misjudged the bend and flew off the track, somersaulting twice and landing upside down.

No one was hurt as I put it back on the Scalextric track!

Louise Foy (11)

DANCING WITH...

All of a sudden I was dancing in space
watching the planets go by.
Then in a flash, I was surrounded by little green men.
They chattered to me in a funny language.
I couldn't understand and I started spinning,
getting dizzy, scared and shaking.
'Wake up or you'll be late.'

Megan Nannfeldt (11)

MURDER IN THE DARK

Felicity was dead, of that we were all quite sure.
There was a clue on the floor, a piece of paper,
which I hoped would lead to the killer.
I'd reached my decision and was waiting for the verdict.
Finally the organiser said,
'You're the winner and here's your prize!'

Karla Thurston (11)

RUN

I ran as fast as I could and still he caught me.
All my friends, or my so-called friends,
had left me behind to suffer the consequences.
I had nowhere else to run except behind the trees.
He crept up and I was . . .
stuck . . . in . . . the . . . mud!

Rebekah Rocker (11)

A MYSTERIOUS TEACHER WITH A DEADLY SECRET

I had been given detention by a mysterious substitute teacher. Beside me was his bag which I peered through. Suddenly I saw a book 'Ancient Rubiyat' which only existed billions of years ago. I reached my hand forward, just then I heard footsteps and the classroom door creaked open . . .

Jay Shetty (11)

THE END OF THE WORLD!

It's so dark and cold, I'm so scared,
I don't know what's going on,
It's only the middle of the morning.
It's the end of the world!
Heeeeee . . . lp!
'Silly Rover, it's only the eclipse,
It can't hurt you, don't worry.'

Deborah Rouse (11)

THE SCENE

Suddenly I heard a noise approaching me, getting louder and louder. Then I turned my head, as the hinges compressed and the attic door opened. I laid my head in my hands and gasped with horror, then a voice groaned, 'Andrew, it's dinner time and stop reading those horror stories...'

Andrew Oduro Ayim (11)

THE CAVE

Najara was told by her mother not to go into the cave.
She was so curious that she went into the cave the next day.
There was this frightening sound like a ghost.
She ran out as fast as her legs could carry her, shaking.

Joanna Odei Frimpong (11)

NIGHTMARE

I'm in my room on a spooky night
My dog is howling, CDs are playing
I hear a creak, a cough, a sneeze
Footsteps are coming closer
The door opens
The light comes on
I scream and close my eyes
It's my dad asking 'Where's my slippers?'

Timothy Gibson (11)

Vahawk

Long ago in the place called China,
there lived a boy, his name was Vahawk.
He was nearly twelve.
He lived alone.
One day a rattlesnake came up to him
with a ring and bit him, he wasn't hurt.
This ring had magical powers.
He was known as Boathon.

Joel Williams (11)

YOU WILL NEVER SEE YOUR MOTHER AGAIN

'You're under arrest! You will never see your mother again.'
I was dumbfounded.
'But . . . I'm . . . only eleven!'
'Yes . . . that's what they all say,' laughed the large policeman very heartily.
Suddenly a red-faced policeman rushed in.
'Sorry . . . wrong girl . . . she's only eleven, sorry . . . mistake due to computer error,' he said sheepishly.

Ayodele Cameron (11)

THE DEAD END

I could feel the dagger plunging through my heart,
I looked back but kept running.
I could see the blood pouring.
I ran into the garden shed
Thinking he didn't see me.
But he did. *'No!'* I screamed.
'Kerry, when will you ever put that book down?'

Kerry McKenzie (11)

THE SEA MONSTER

I was going further into the sea, the cold water tingled on my hips.
Suddenly something grabbed my ankle pulling me under.
My throat was dry with fear.
Before I could do anything, a spluttering, laughing little brother emerged from the water.
'Oh Scott you little monster,' I laughed.

Lisa Clavey (11)

THE ECLIPSE

Tension was mounting,
everyone was excited,
lots of people were with me on that cliff,
they all looked funny in their protective glasses.

Suddenly it fell quiet,
everyone looked up,
oohs and aahs were all that could be heard.

Then it went dark,
it was nothing other than the eclipse!

Carly Forster (11)

THEY'RE OUT

They stood in a perfect circle.
She felt an air of anticipation, she knew all eyes were on her.
She concentrated her thoughts on the ring of flickering lights before her.
She inhaled deeply feeling her lungs expand.
She blew energetically . . .
They were out.
The birthday candles were out.

Siobhan Hughes (11)

FINAL MOMENTS

I knew that I would die without it
but it was going and there was nothing
anyone could do to stop it.

More people came, looked at me, I looked back.
The darkness swept over me -
the solar eclipse of August '99,
I'll never forget it.

Jack Robinson (11)

BURGLED OR NOT!

She walked to the front door, it was open, had she been burgled or not?
She could hear rustling, she didn't dare put the light on . . .
She crept into the room, then the lights went on.
'Happy birthday!' shouted all of her family together.

Eleanor Jane Hopkins (11)

DESPERATE TO GO

I braced myself. This wasn't going to be easy.
I imagined the thousands of faces staring at me,
laughing at me.
My heart began to pound but I knew I had to do it.
I raised a shaky hand into the air.
'Please Miss, can I go to the toilet?'

Stephanie Jayson (11)

APPROACH WITH CAUTION

I approached with caution.
The screams of its victims could be heard
along with the clanking of metal.
My heart thudded in my chest as I
grew nearer to my fate.
I sat down prepared for what lay ahead . . .
Yes! I survived the fastest roller-coaster in the world!

Michaela McQueeney (11)

TROUBLE

There I was, in-between two well-built guards.
They each had one of my arms tightly held.
I walked along with them at the same speed,
so I wouldn't get into any more trouble.
I was silent as we got nearer, then a door opened -
the head teacher didn't look happy.

Samantha Lustig (11)

ON THE FIELD

A murderous look in her eyes, Lisa stared down the field.
Lisa watched them coming, running, they were coming closer
and they were chasing Samantha.
Lisa started running, Samantha was a metre away,
Lisa dived and Samantha was grounded.
Lisa grabbed the rugby ball and passed to Emily.
Mission complete.

Georgina Whitehead (11)

RAGING SEAS

Raging seas toss the boat up and down like a cork.
Howling gales scream like manic wolves on a hunt.
Passengers and crew alike are terrified.
Suddenly we hit a smooth, high cliff,
we're sinking, sinking slowly.
Terrific thunder roars out a final message.
Get out of that bath - now!

Timothy Scargill (11)

NERVOUS

A week before I was going back to school
I was really nervous.
We were going to have some tests,
I hadn't revised.
What if I get low marks?
I kept thinking to myself.
Now it's all over.
I've taken them and I've got the results.
I did fine.

Sarah Sultana (11)

NEAR-DEATH EXPERIENCE

I kept still, rigid, as explosions split the night.
People were dying right in front of me.
I knew I had to move or die.
I started to edge towards the open doorway behind me.
Suddenly everything went black.
The last thing I heard was,
'I said, computer off *now!*'

Andrew Barklam (11)

FEARS

I had always been a coward,
scared of anything and everything
but I had to face my fears.
I climbed into the enormous object
and was raised high into the sky,
then tipped and tossed.
Finally I swooped down and stopped,
'That ride was okay, let's have another go?'

Emily Brown (11)

ECLIPSE

3, 2, 1 - it's started, the first total eclipse in Britain since 1927.
There are investigations going on in some places.
It was starting to feel cool, it was dull.
There was only fourteen minutes until totality.
As the street lights came on, people started to feel eerie,
and finally totality.

Matthew Mullen (11)

CHINA'S FIRST IMPRESSION OF THE ECLIPSE

The dragon wakes and flexes its claws.
It stares up at the sun: its prey.
It leaps into the sky and ascends up to the fireball
flickering helplessly above.
Its jaws part and it engulfs the sun in his mouth.
Totality swamps the Earth.

Emma Chandley (11)

GOING TO THE DENTIST

There I was in the waiting room
thinking with great fear.
'We are ready' a voice said.
We entered the room and sat down.
There were people fussing over me
as if I was really important.
I felt a sharp prick.
Everything went blurred.
as my mum's face faded away.

Helen Alexander (11)

ON THE RUN

As I crouch in a cramped hole, I feel the cold creeping up my spine. My heart skips a beat. The figure comes closer, his cold eyes searching. He disappears from view. It's now or never. I dash out, as fast as my legs will carry me.

'Home, I win!'

Siân Humphries (11)

No Escaping

The time had come, the time I had been dreading ever since I visited that terrifying building that very morning. There was no escaping it now. I watched as before my very eyes a yellow substance was poured menacingly onto the familiar spoon. Nooooo . . .

Gulp! Yuck, how I hate medicine.

Fiona Kelly (11)

MYSTERIOUS FOOTSTEPS

You're walking on a cold, misty morning when crunching footsteps approach behind you. You quicken your pace, but the footsteps speed up too, then suddenly, someone grabs you. They tie a rope around you and pull you down, down . . . then you awake, sweating, to discover it was only a dream.

Hannah Tickle (11)

THE KILLING

'Don't shoot me, don't kill me!'
The excited boy saw the wild expression on the face of the victim.
There was a sudden flash of light in front of him . . . silence.
The boy smirked very proudly and triumphantly turned off the computer.

Joanne Allen (11)

FISHING

I've been here for an hour,
I've cast in again but still no fish.
It's begun to rain.
The bank's become slippery.
At last a bite.
I pull and pull.
I keep slipping, I can't land the fish.
Oh no, it's got away.
With a little laugh it swims away.

Bernice Connell (11)

WINTER

As I woke up I looked at my clock,
it was 6.30am and it was dark.
I knew something special was going on, but what?
Silently I crept downstairs hoping not to wake anyone.
I opened the door and I knew what it was.

Christmas!

Kayleigh Nash (11)

THE SHUTTLECOCK CATASTROPHE

There it was, staring at us with evil glowing eyes,
fangs as sharp as steel, claws curled and clasping.
It pounced, I dived but it had its prey,
dragging it into the cobwebby darkness.
I tried to save it, but my shuttlecock was gone forever.
Grandma's cat had eaten it.

Ian Copeland (11)

KIDNAPPED

The busy people loomed overhead.
Tears were rolling down my cheeks,
nobody would notice me down here.
I ran around in a circle, all hot and flustered.
Someone had wrapped their arms around me -
I'm being kidnapped!
Hang on -
I know that perfume.
It's my mum!

Amy Briggs (11)

TIGER TROUBLE

The tiger's golden skin stood out
against the silvery green grass.
His eyes glared at me.
I started to run.
It started to run as well.
I dived to the rocky ground.
The tiger saw me, it pounced
and that was the last thing I saw.

Andrew Barrett (11)

THE MONSTER THAT ATE THE SUN

The giant shadow creeps across the ground, the monster is coming. It opens its huge mouth and closes it over the sun. We dance and yell and fire our arrows into the sky. The moon slides away from the sun, the monster is gone . . . the eclipse is over.

Stephen Mitchell (11)

FOOTSTEPS

Ann could hear footsteps behind her as she was walking to her car after work. She ran as fast as she could, knowing that someone was following her. She thought that she would never reach her car, she was wrong. She did reach her car, she just didn't reach it alive.

Rachel Price (11)

MYSTERY OF THE DEEP

I could clearly see the dark, shadowy outline looming towards me, moving smoothly and swiftly through the brightly coloured corals. The huge, heavy breathing, the bubbles floating up towards the sunlit surface. The shadow was closing in on me and then the diver appeared from the emerald green seaweed.

Peter Willis (11)

SCARED OF WATER?

Whoosh! A wave of water flowed over my head. I coughed as I gulped a mouthful of air, it was happening again. I couldn't take it anymore. My heart was pounding as the current was pushing me under. I looked up, 'Shall we go on the ride again?'

Catherine Porter (11)

A Cold Touch

I stood at the old wooden door with tears in my eyes, shaking all over, my heart thumping loudly. I took a deep breath, stepped forward a few paces and instantly started to twist the doorknob. A cold shiver ran up my spine . . . as the producer touched my shoulder.

Rachael Hilderley

THE ROSE

'Carrie, keep this to remember me.' Lisa gave Carrie a white rose. She got on the train, 'Goodbye, Carrie.'
'Ow!' Carried exclaimed, 'that hurt.'
She looked down at her finger, it started to change shape and colour, so did the rest of her. She was changing into a beautiful unicorn.

Rhiannon Burgess (11)

THE MOST AMAZING EXPERIENCE OF OUR LIFE

I was running and running through the fields of wheat in the lazy warmth of the sun, with Lassie not far behind me. I couldn't stop , not now. Thank God, I reached the commotion and squeezed through the crowds. I looked up. The total eclipse. 'What an experience, Lassie.'

Beccy Rolland (11)

CARELESSNESS

The boulder hit it. I watched with horror and fear. It fell, gathering speed, yet everything in slow motion. Flashing colours, green and blue, tumbling downwards, spiralling round.

Crash! Splintered, devastated, pieces lying everywhere.

'Never play with balls indoors. Look at my vase, smashed to smithereens!' shouted Mum tearfully.

Emily Read (11)

THE DEMON FROM THE DARK SIDE

The Gods called out to me, warning me that whoever went to kill the Demon never came back.

I prepared myself to defeat the Dark Side. I was ready.

I found him staring at me with his glowing eyes. Before I could draw my sword, he had turned me to stone.

Emily Cawston-Rollin (11)

MINI SAGA

It was coming right at me. I had to get ready to catch it. It had been there for days, ever since I let it out, and now it had to go back. Getting ready for impact, three, two, one . . . 'Oh Sam,' I said, 'you scared my rabbit.'

Charlotte Burton (11)

SHADOWS

There it was, lurking in the darkness beneath the shadows. The rustlings and the snapping of twigs caused rodents to disappear. Suddenly, a pair of bright eyes appeared out of the undergrowth. There was a squawk and a flapping of wings and a piercing voice that said, 'Dinner, Felix!'

Harriet Newcombe (11)

COLD-BLOODED KILLER

I crept upstairs, then I felt a hand on my shoulder even colder than metal. The woman's nails dug into my skin like ice. She breathed the words, 'Just do as I say,' into my ear. Quickly, I took the full rubbish bag from my mother and put it outside.

Cara George (11)

WORRIES

My hand trembled as I picked the dreadful brown thing up and passed it to my mum. I was positive that what was inside would be terrible. Mum frowned and fingered it open. It fell out. I closed my eyes, dreading the worst but . . . my school report wasn't too bad.

Bryannie Drury (11)

RUNNING, RUNNING

I ran faster and faster through the pits of hell. I could feel the heat rising all around me. I ran, there was no escape. I heard someone scream, then someone say, 'Wake up, wake up!' So I did, it was just a dream.

Roxanne Evans (11)

MINI SAGA

A faint sound was heard. It echoed around the open room, a cackle of laughter came through the cracks in the door. It got louder, and louder. Each time, I got more tense. The door flew open and footsteps came towards me. 'Did you hear that joke?' chuckled my sister.

Kelly Parkhouse (11)

THE WARM PRESENCE

As I smelt the air, a sudden tingling ran down my spine. Something was behind me. I turned around, all I could see was a dark, black shadow coming towards me with a knife. I started to run down the stairs, but I slipped. 'Aaagh!' Someone pushed me.

Hayley Dixon (11)

FEROCIOUS MONSTER

The ferocious monster jumped on my head, clawing me till I bled.
'Get off, get off!' I screamed.
Her black fur stood up straight, which meant she was angry. Her green eyes glared at me hungrily.
'Get your stupid cat out of my room!' I shouted at my little sister.

Nicola Kirby (11)

THAT BOOK!

Someone was following me. I was too scared to turn around. I froze.
There were footsteps getting closer and closer, louder and louder.
'Boo!'
'Wow, what a nightmare. I'll never read those thrillers again.'
She picked up the book from her bedside table and tossed it into the bin.

Laura Gatehouse (11)

THE RACE

There wasn't far to go,
I heard cheering.
The rain poured down.
Something was pushing me on,
something unknown.
I looked behind me,
... nothing.
I looked to the sides,
... nothing.
The chequered flag flapped as I passed it,
I had won!

'Would you turn that PlayStation off!'
Mum called.

Karl Hayman (11)

THE GARGOYLE

I entered the ancient chapel. The smell of fear wafted on a chilling breeze. I stopped, stone-cold, in dread of the hideous beast which sat before me. It lifted its tortuous limbs and hissed. A putrid smell made me back away. It lunged forward, mouth open. Death ensued.

Cherith Webb (11)

THE VICTIM

He glared at me, pupils dilated, panting in terror.

He sidled towards the door, head shaking violently, fingers groping for escape. I stepped in the way, pushing him back. 'Look,' I hissed, 'You've got . . .'
'No, no!' screamed my little brother, 'I won't clean out the rabbits!'

Tamsyn Lee (11)

ON THE BACK OF A HAWK

I was flying swiftly on the back of a hawk. We glided past the reflective moon, past the planets - Mercury, Mars and Venus, even a comet with its fiery tail.

It was so real, but the comet made me jump and I awoke from my deep slumber.

Victoria Evans (11)

The Earthquake

It was three in the morning and I was fast asleep in my bed, when suddenly the room started shaking. I opened my eyes and was consumed with fear as the ceiling came crashing down on me.

Hours later, I opened my eyes and saw life for the last time.

Cassie Specterman (11)

THE SHOT

There she was, the last ten seconds. It all depended on her, the score nine-nine. The sun was shining brightly, the wind against her. Five seconds, she knew what to do. She took it. Yes! The teacher shouted, 'Good shot, but you're goal defence!' The netball team had lost.

Lauren Webster (11)

Mini Saga

At last I could see the finishing line. My legs were aching and throbbing like mad. I got nearer and nearer to the finishing line. Then suddenly, I tripped over. I tried to get up, but I couldn't, and suddenly it came to me. I had lost the race.

Aiza Arshad (11)

SUDDENLY COME... SUDDENLY GONE?

It has come suddenly. Humungous, spherical and the most brightest, dazzling white. It had little grooves all over the mysterious object. The ants stood, unable to move. The grass shook and a tremendous blow fell upon the sphere, which was then launched into space. 'Well done, son, hole in one.'

Jennifer Coughlin (11)

MY MINI SAGA

I walked into my room and saw them sat there, sat there reading my personal diary that I'd written all my private thoughts in every day, and they were sat there, sat there reading it out loud. I nearly died. They were on the page entitled 'The worst day of my life'!

Francesca Blake (11)

ECLIPSED

Everywhere went dark. What was it? As I sat down and turned the TV on, the pictures were of total darkness. What was I thinking? When everywhere was silent and cold, the sun was no longer out. It must have been the total eclipse. It was amazing!

Nealey Swadkins (11)

THE BAR

I look at a brown, rusty bar, wondering what I'm supposed to do with it. Orderless, isolated and confused. What is it? What am I supposed to do? I pick it up, it melts in my hands. I like it. It's sweet . . .it's chocolate!

Rosie Dymock (11)

THE RISING MONSTER

The coffin lid lifted as Dracula arose and looked me in the eye. I ran to the door, but it was no use, it was locked. I tripped and stumbled as I headed for the stairs, gazing at this horrific monster. My head lifted from the pillow. I'd been dreaming.

Christopher Baker (11)

MINI SAGA

Thunderclouds bellowed in the distant valley. Suddenly, the door swung open and a stranger stomped in. Echoes ran through my head as he slammed the door shut. His bloodshot eyes glared at me. He had a large figure, he was broad-shouldered and tall. He handed me a notice reading 'Rent due.'

Ayesha Malik (11)

THE CHALLENGE

She'd started now, she had to finish. No time for hesitation, not at this point. A mask of determination and agony streaked her face. 'Just a little bit further . . .' she panted. Her muscles shrieked with exhaustion as with one last mighty heave, she emerged from the covers of her bed.

Elizabeth Williams (11)

BETRAYAL

My hands reached up to the cupboard. Fingers tingling, I grabbed it, looked around, then ran for my life! Droplets of sweat slid down my face. Only when I was back in my room did I dare look at it. I shoved it in my mouth, my brother's last chocolate!

Zoë Copson (11)

TENSE MOMENTS

I jogged through the town - only a few blocks to go. The church clock struck 8:30, time was running out. I quickened my pace. I had to get there in time. My heart beat faster as I turned the final corner - and arrived at school just in time for assembly.

John DeBoo (11)

THE MYSTERIOUS FIGURE

Big, ponderous steps thundered up the hallway. I froze in fear as an enormous figure appeared at my bedroom doorway. Piercing blue eyes stared at me as the mysterious figure entered my brightly coloured room. I smiled as I realised it was my Dad, who bellowed 'Tidy your room!'

Danielle Lowis (11)

MY SISTER NEEDS HELP!

My sister was hurt on the floor. I tried helping her, but it was no use. I rang my nanna and she came round to our house. Eventually, we got Kelly downstairs and got her a cup of tea, then we all made sure Kelly was all right and said goodnight.

Rebecca Wall (11)

A Glimpse Of The Beastie

I was just rounding up my sheep, aye, was then I saw it. Three humps rose up from the loch, behind the castle they were. Surprised as I was, its head rose, the eyes staring at me, cold yet kind. It stared, then drifted back, back to the water . . .

Paul Harrison (11)

THE BATTLE OF THE MIDDLE AGES

He was to lead the bloodiest battle there ever was.
They walked onto the field of the most feared.
He ordered the army to charge.
He stood high with his sword full length in front.
The enemy fired, he was struck in the eye.
And was the first one down.

Michael Myers (11)

TEARS IN MY EYES

I couldn't believe I actually did it. Should I have? Yes? No? I'd tried before but just cried in agony. Yes! I was going to do it. I plunged down the huge carving knife! Tears rapidly rolled down my hot cheeks. I cried out in anguish . . .

The onions are ready!

Kerry Taplin (11)

Paradise

I braced myself,
I was ready, ready for anything.
My enemy was pacing up and down,
Guarding the door to paradise.
I had to get in somehow, and quick.
It was then that I had the idea.
I picked myself up and charged through the door.
Finally I had chocolate.

Jennifer Baldwin (11)

Fair Dues

Sitting there, motionless,
Waiting for the master,
to step onto my territory.
Then, suddenly,
He brings out the relic.
It has been silently rotting
in the depths of that pocket for years.
This is it,
The hand-over
The receiving of . . .

My pocket money!

Alison Seal (11)

IN THE KITCHEN

I could hear him unsheathing his knife,
It was his daily mission,
I heard the sound of the knife,
Like a saw,
Bang . . . ! Bang!
The thud of metal on wood.
I sat down on the edge of my seat,
He entered the room . . .
'Anyone want a double cheese sandwich?'

Nadia Schramm (11)

THE HALT

Like a speeding train down the road it came, bounding. No thought for what may be in its path. It carried on running as if there was no time to stop. Then with a sudden halt, right in front of me, there he stood. My faithful companion, Herman, my dog.

Faye-Marie Cryer (11)

THE DENTIST

Waiting, waiting for the moment of truth. Sitting, sitting on the edge of my seat. Breathing, breathing so hard my insides ache. I can hardly bear the intensity. What will they do to me when I travel through the doors of fate? Will I need a filling?

Kathryn McCandless (11)

BEDROOM HORROR

Hand shaking; mind flicking through all the things that had happened over the last few weeks. I clutched the handle, opened the door, there they were! The smelliest things ever seen, a dirty musty aroma filled the room. I put on my gloves and put my socks in the wash.

Kathryn Elizabeth Callow (10)

DON'T LET THE SUN GET IN YOUR EYES, DON'T LET THE CLOUDS BREAK YOUR HEART

The world awaited the special event.

The cars clogged the roads with their glum grey smoke as everyone journeyed down to the foot of the land.

All the news updates and weather summaries shared in the anticipation.

Ah well, stick around till 2090, perhaps the clouds won't block that eclipse!

Diarmuid Tejero-White (11)

JEWELS!

As I crept into the dark I saw jewels glimmering, old books, documents, statues, ancient garments and paintings, hundreds of them. Old, possibly worth money. I picked some jewels up, they were heavy. Then I heard it . . .
'Have you finished tidying your bedroom, Naomi?' my mum said.

Naomi Crewe (11)

ECLIPSE

People were dazzled by the sparkling diamond atmosphere of the gleaming disc that had been devoured by the moon. The wildlife was confused and everybody was brimming with excitement and enthusiasm. All the locals stopped to view it. Then everyone looked as it slowly slid away.

Thomas Zacharchenko (11)

WAITING FOR THE CHANCE

There he was. He could not see me but I could see him. He passed so close, I thought he would hear my heart thumping. He stopped, looked around, then walked on. This is my chance. I stepped out into the open and ran as fast as I could, *'Home Tree!'*

Deborah Lomax (11)

A Madman's Obsession

His objective was to accomplish a daring task using only one match. He'd screwed up once before and would not let it happen again. This time he would finish the job off. He struck the match with fury. This time the birthday candles had been lit and not the tablecloth.

Ben Fish (11)

ANGST

I couldn't bear the thought of having to go back there. Finally, I plucked up enough courage and set off. When I got there I took my last breath of freedom for the next seven hours.

'Good morning ' said my teacher as I started another term of torture.

Nazneen Tabassum (11)

THE DREADED MOMENT

There was a deadly silence
in the classroom.
A sickening feeling,
filled the pit of my stomach.
It seemed every vein in my body
had frozen - I couldn't move or speak.
My face glowed a deep scarlet.
Then came the moment I'd been
dreading - my exam results.
'. . . Nadia Yousuf, A+,'
Relief!

Nadia Yousuf (11)

SPLASH!

Violent waves hit the ship like a battering ram.
'All hands on deck!' shouted Captain Jack. Lightning struck *zzzzap!* The ship's mast set on fire. Ferocious waves hit the deck as men were carried off to sea.
'Save us,' they screamed.
'Get out of the bath now, Jamie,' Mum shouted.

Jamie Linnell (11)

STRANGELY FAMILIAR

He walked into the cold, dimly-lit room. He remembered the familiar carvings cut into the wood. As the door thundered behind him, his spine shivered. He remembered the horrid smells, then, a kind small hand took his and pulled.
'Come on, Dad, we'll be late to meet the teacher.'

David Kelley (11)

TO MY SURPRISE

It was an intense moment on
my favourite soap,
when out of the corner of my eye
a shadow went past my window.
Although I knew nothing could get in
I sat trembling with fear, a chill ran down my spine.
I jumped, it was the biggest spider I'd ever seen.

Hayley Sharman (11)

A Tiger's Teatime

I saw the tiger ripping the deer limb from limb. I heard the flesh tear as the blood oozed from the open wound. It made my skin crawl as the tiger crunched the fragile bones. Suddenly my mum came in and switched the TV off.
'Time for tea,' she said.

Corrine Kaenzig (11)

THE NIGHTLY MENACE

I lay there, waiting, waiting for it to start.

Like it was the night before.

Then, it started, the deafening *squeak, squeak, squeak,* the non-stop *rustle, rustle, rustle,* the sickly *thud, thud, thud.*

Cowering under my quilt, I couldn't take any more.

'Bubbles, you silly hamster, get off your wheel!'

Sara Bentley (11)

THE KISS

There he was, my idol, Brad Pitt,
standing alone by a tree.
Cautiously I walked towards him,
hoping he wouldn't disappear.
His blue eyes stared into space.
I reached up, closed my eyes and
kissed him on the cheek.
A camera flashed.
He remained motionless.
Yuk! I kissed a waxwork!

Laura Saggars (11)

THE STAR

My eyes are red from crying. I kiss your lips once more and prepare myself for loneliness. The night will be long without you. It will be hard to sleep tonight. When my room is decorated, your poster will go up on my wall.

I love you Scott from Five.

Leah Mann (11)

RAZOR BLADES

I could see razor blades chopping through the
air in circles.
Sweat poured down my head,
I felt my legs begin to weaken.
I could hear screaming,
hollering,
my heart pounding,
I felt the breeze from the fan cool me,
after the long, hard bike race.

Charlotte Low (11)

THE SOUND OF WATER

The water's gurgle grew louder -
enjoying its freedom.

Usually contained
It ran freely in every direction.
A trickle at first, it increased
In speed and volume!

Gurgling with excitement,
Carelessly splashing.
Fiercely determined, pushing away
Obstacles in its path!

Water closed round my feet -
I'd left the bath taps running!

Charlotte Shannon-Little (11)

SUDDEN DARKNESS

As darkness engulfed us
And, the diminishing light ebbed away,
The accursed ceased jesting about their position.
The huelessness caused an unnatural quiet
To hang, like a cloud, over the sable room,
Generating an unnerving atmosphere.
A sudden jolt caused superstition to flow;
No, hamsters don't like moving houses!

Hannah Clark (11)

Mini Saga

The race was on! As I shifted into third gear and went easily round the first bend the second car drew nearer. I made the sharp corner pretty well for an amateur. As I changed into fifth gear the car stopped and the screen went blank. My PlayStation was broken!

Michael Addinell (11)

Honk

His grotesque features protruded from his pale, paper-thin face. His eyes, defined with black; his lips, scarlet as blood. The fresh sawdust, crisp under broad feet, his arm, pale and thin under purple tunic, reached up, up, up -
'Honk,' hooted the clown's red nose. He grinned.

Rhiannon Byers (11)

LOVE

She was in love.
He didn't love her.
So one day she went to talk to him.
What would she say?
That she needed him?
How would she say that she loved him?
She walked up to him, she opened her mouth, and said:
'Miaow!'
Two cats walked away together.

Rachel Krengel (11)

The Shadow!

Perched on the cool rocks, gazing at the sun's blazing beams; blinking on the rippling sea waves, I was enveloped in an enchanting aura! Suddenly . . . a chilling shadow fingered over me, encasing me like a shroud! Dread clutched my heart . . . as something gave me a start . . . Seagull's poo!

Georgiana Simmons (11)

ALL IS NOT WHAT IT SEEMS . . .

'You will bow down and respect me.'
I stood tall, 'Never' I snarled, 'you may be king, but you are also my enemy!'
'You show disrespect,' he said flatly, 'you will die!'
I brandished my sword, 'No, you will die!'
Slice!
A tongue lolled, a head rolled.
Applause. The curtain descended.

Shelley Greenwood (11)

ALTERNATE EXERCISE

I tried to stay calm
but I was hurtling through the air,
pulled by a powerful force.
Whizzing past the blurred lamp posts,
my heart beating ever faster,
I finally stopped at our gate.
Straightening my hair,
I thought to myself
'Next time, I'll get my
sister to walk the dog!'

Elissa Rose (11)

ALONE IN THE DARK

I was now trapped in the old, abandoned house which stood gloomily in Albert Lane.
I could hear strange sounds all around me.
The front door through which I had entered had locked itself behind me.
All was lost . . . then *something* appeared, a, a . . .
'PlayStation switched off, please,' said Mum. 'Bedtime.'

Liam Paul Murphy (11)

THE BATTLE

We pushed through the mass of enemies, running, shoving. Eager to get what we wanted. A team going out to battle, prepared to kill if necessary. There might be bloodshed and tears, but it would be worth it. Yelling, we leapt onto the back seat of the coach. *Victory!*

Charlotte Hawksley (11)